DISNEY · PIXAR

FIVE TALES
FROM THE
ROAD

Dear Parent:

Congratulations! Your child is taking the first steps on an exciting journey. The destination? Independent reading!

STEP INTO READING® will help your child get there. The program offers five steps to reading success. Each step includes fun stories and colorful art. There are also Step into Reading Sticker Books, Step into Reading Math Readers, Step into Reading Phonics Readers, Step into Reading Write-In Readers, and Step into Reading Phonics Boxed Sets—a complete literacy program with something for every child.

Learning to Read, Step by Step!

Ready to Read   Preschool–Kindergarten
• big type and easy words • rhyme and rhythm • picture clues
For children who know the alphabet and are eager to begin reading.

Reading with Help   Preschool–Grade 1
• basic vocabulary • short sentences • simple stories
For children who recognize familiar words and sound out new words with help.

Reading on Your Own   Grades 1–3
• engaging characters • easy-to-follow plots • popular topics
For children who are ready to read on their own.

Reading Paragraphs   Grades 2–3
• challenging vocabulary • short paragraphs • exciting stories
For newly independent readers who read simple sentences with confidence.

Ready for Chapters   Grades 2–4
• chapters • longer paragraphs • full-color art
For children who want to take the plunge into chapter books but still like colorful pictures.

STEP INTO READING® is designed to give every child a successful reading experience. The grade levels are only guides. Children can progress through the steps at their own speed, developing confidence in their reading, no matter what their grade.

Remember, a lifetime love of reading starts with a single step!

STEP INTO READING®

Disney · PIXAR

FIVE TALES
FROM THE
ROAD

Step 1 and 2 Books

A Collection of Five Early Readers

Random House 🏠 New York

Contents

RACE AROUND THE WORLD

By Susan Amerikaner

Illustrated by the Disney Storybook Artists

Random House 🏠 New York

Lightning is a race car.

He is fast!

Lightning is a big star.

A car from Italy
is fast, too.

Who is faster?

The cars will race!

The first race is
in Japan.

The car from Italy
is the winner.

Lightning is not happy.

The second race is in Italy.

Both cars want
to win!

One car spins

on the track!

Lightning wins!

The third race is
in Radiator Springs.
It is the last race.

The cars line up.

The fans are ready.

The cars race!

The fans cheer.

Go, Lightning, go!

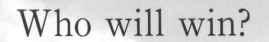

Who will win?

DISNEY · PIXAR

Cars 2

SECRET
AGENT
MATER

By Melissa Lagonegro

Illustrated by Caroline LaVelle Egan,
Andrew Phillipson, Scott Tilley,
and Seung Beom Kim

Random House 🏠 New York

Mater is a spy car.

Spies catch bad cars.

Spies have
secret meetings.

Spies fight bad cars.

<u>Hi-ya!</u>

Finn is a spy car,
too.
Mater helps him.

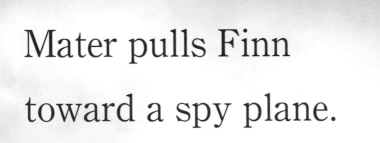

Mater pulls Finn
toward a spy plane.

Mater learns secrets.

Mater goes undercover.

Mater tricks
the bad cars.
He finds clues!

Mater soars away
from the bad cars!

Mater is trapped!

Mater escapes!

He and his friends
are in danger.

Mater and Lightning race
down the street.
Holley helps them.

Mater and Lightning fly!

Mater solves the case!

Mater is a hero!

SUPER SPIES

By Susan Amerikaner

Illustrated by Caroline LaVelle Egan, Scott Tilley,
Andrew Phillipson, and Seung Beom Kim

Random House 🏠 New York

Lightning McQueen is
on a plane.
He is going
to a big race.

Mater is going,
too.

He will help Lightning.

Finn and Holley

are spy cars.

Bad cars try
to hurt race cars.
Finn and Holley
must stop them.

Holley calls Mater
at the race.
Mater likes Holley.
He leaves
to meet her.

Mater sees the bad cars.

Finn fights them!

Mater is not there
to help Lightning.
Lightning loses the race!

Lightning is mad
at Mater.

Mater wants
to go home.

The bad cars follow him
to the airport.
Finn will help!

Finn and Mater race away
from the bad cars.
Finn fights the bad cars.

Mater drives
into the spy plane.
Holley waits for him.
They will escape!

Holley and Finn
tell Mater
they are spy cars.

They think Mater
is a spy car, too.
Mater will help
find the bad cars.

Holley gives Mater
spy tools.
She dresses him up
to fool the bad cars.

Now Mater
is a spy car,
too!

Mater finds

the bad cars.

They want
to hurt Lightning!

Mater tries
to warn Lightning.
But Lightning does
not see him.

The bad cars catch
Finn, Holley, and Mater.
They trap them
in a big clock.

Mater gets away!

Holley escapes,
too!

She fights the bad cars.

Mater finds Lightning.
They race away
from the bad cars.

Mater uses
his spy tools.

He and Lightning

fly up

in the air.

Mater and Lightning
go to see
the Queen.

Mater helped
Finn and Holley
stop the bad cars.
The Queen thanks him.

Mater and Lightning
are heroes!

DISNEY · PIXAR
Cars

MATER'S
BIRTHDAY SURPRISE

By Melissa Lagonegro
Illustrated by the Disney Storybook Artists

Random House 🏠 New York

It is Mater's birthday.
His friends
are planning
a surprise party.

It is a secret!

Lightning is in charge.

Everyone gets a job.

Luigi blows up balloons.

He uses his tire pump.

Guido makes

a pretend tire cake.

Fillmore makes a batch
of his tasty fuel.
Mater loves it.

Jeff Gorvette races
to the party.
He does not want
to be late.

Lightning sets up
the party games.
Mater loves games.

He likes

Pin the Bumper

on the Car.

Sally wraps presents.
Mater wants
a new tow hook
and a rusty hubcap.

Flo picks out
streamers and bows.
Red uses his ladder
to hang them.

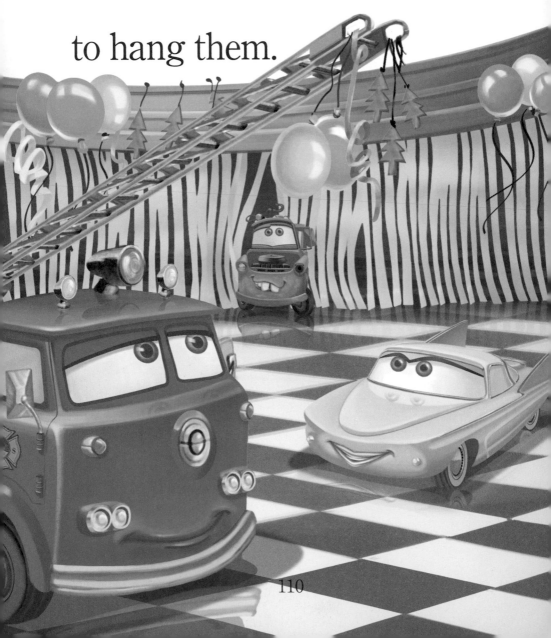

Ramone paints
a birthday sign.

Mater's friends arrive!
Sarge leads them
to the party.

They are very quiet.
They don't want Mater
to hear them.

Finn and Holley come
for the party!

They are on

a top-secret mission.

They bring Mater

a new disguise.

The party begins!

Presents are piled up.

Streamers hang down.

Mater is coming!

The cars hide!

Lightning looks

for Mater.

Surprise!

It is not Mater!

It is Lizzie.

She has the party hats.

Where is Mater?

Lightning goes
to find him.
He looks
around town.

Sheriff looks,
too.
He searches
the back roads.

Lightning and Sheriff

come back

to the party.

They could not
find Mater.

Where is he?

Surprise!
Mater switches off
his new
present disguise.

His friends are
surprised instead.

Mater had fun
tricking his friends.

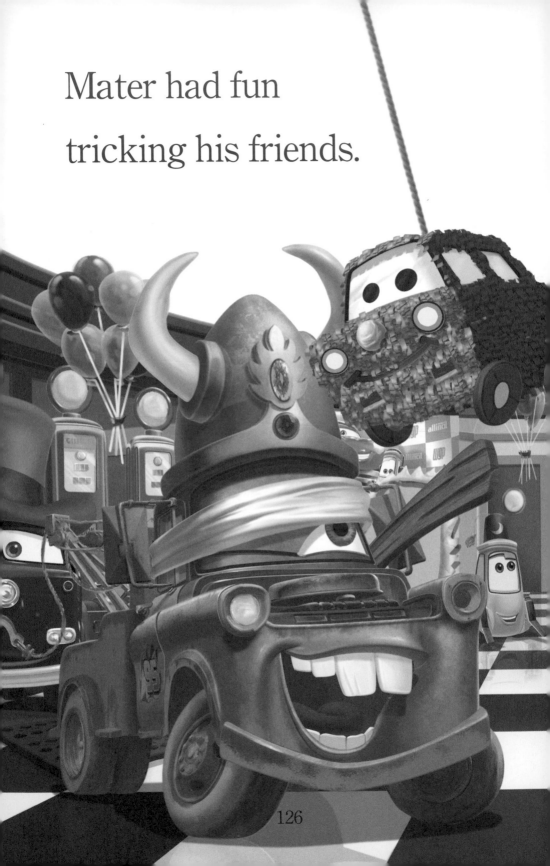

But he has
even more fun
at his party.
He plays games.

Happy birthday, Mater!

DISNEY·PIXAR
Cars

Mater
and the
Little Tractors

Adapted by Chelsea Eberly

Illustrated by Andy Phillipson,
Scott Tilley, David Boelke, and
the Disney Storybook Artists

Random House 🏠 New York

One morning,
Mater was making
a music box.

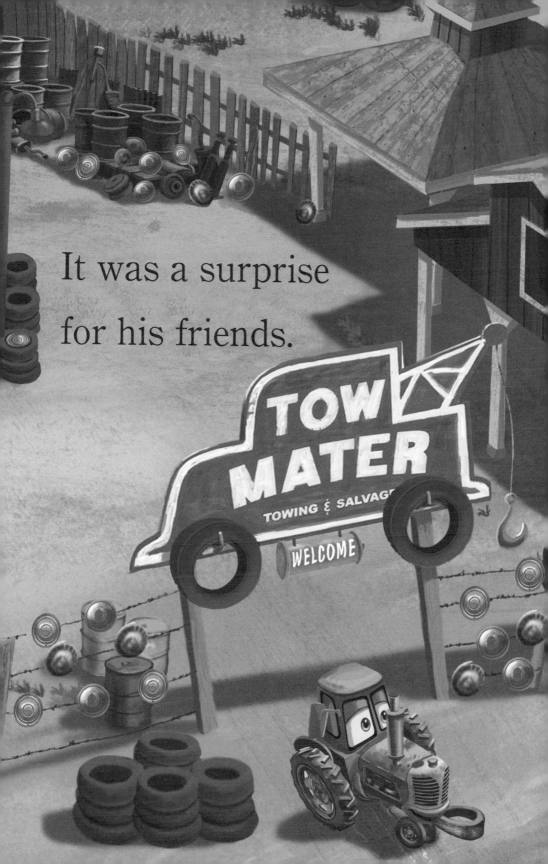

It was a surprise
for his friends.

The music box
was done!
Mater hooked it
to his towline.
He headed
to Main Street.

Mater showed
the music box
to Ramone.
Ramone was
too busy to look.

A little tractor
was painting
his shop!

135

Mater showed
the music box
to Lightning McQueen.
Lightning was busy.
He was chasing
a runaway tractor.

Mater took

the music box

to Luigi's tire shop.

Luigi was busy,
too.

A little tractor
had knocked over
a tower of tires!

Mater took
the music box
to Red.

Red was crying.
Little tractors
had crushed
his flowers!

Mater took
the music box
to Sheriff.

Sheriff could not
look at it.
He had
to catch
the little tractors!

The little tractors
were everywhere!
One was using
Ramone's paint.

One was playing

with Red's flowers.

One was eating

Luigi's tires.

The little tractors
were making a mess!

Mater's friends
needed his help.
He had an idea.

Mater turned on
his music box.
A shy little tractor
followed him.

Mater drove slowly
down the street.
More little tractors
followed him.

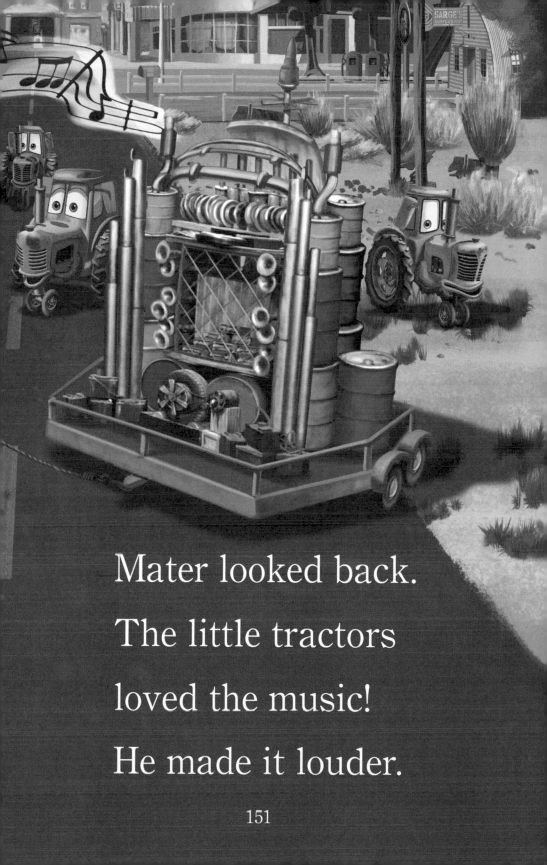

Mater looked back.
The little tractors
loved the music!
He made it louder.

The little tractors
followed the music
into the junkyard.

The fence would keep them inside.

Everyone cheered!

The tractors could not
cause any more trouble.
Sheriff thanked Mater.

The little tractors
danced in circles.
Mater and his friends
watched.
They all had fun.

Mater's music box
had saved the day!